BLOOMSBURY EDUCATION
Bloomsbury Publishing Plc
50 Bedford Square, London, WC1B 3DP, UK
Bloomsbury Publishing Ireland Limited
29 Earlsfort Terrace, Dublin 2, D02 AY28, Ireland

BLOOMSBURY, BLOOMSBURY EDUCATION and the Diana logo are trademarks of Bloomsbury Publishing Plc

First published in Great Britain, 2026 by Bloomsbury Publishing Plc
This edition published in Great Britain,
2026 by Bloomsbury Publishing Plc

Text copyright © Joshua Seigal, 2026
Illustrations copyright © Chris Piascik, 2026

Joshua Seigal and Chris Piascik have asserted their rights under the Copyright, Designs and Patents Act, 1988, to be identified as Author and Illustrator of this work

This is a work of fiction. Names and characters are the product of the author's imagination and any resemblance to actual persons, living or dead, is entirely coincidental.

All rights reserved. No part of this publication may be: i) reproduced or transmitted in any form, electronic or mechanical, including photocopying, recording or by means of any information storage or retrieval system without prior permission in writing from the publishers; or ii) used or reproduced in any way for the training, development or operation of artificial intelligence (AI) technologies, including generative AI technologies. The rights holders expressly reserve this publication from the text and data mining exception as per Article 4(3) of the Digital Single Market Directive (EU) 2019/790

A catalogue record for this book is available from the British Library

ISBN: PB: 978-1-80199-790-4; ePub: 978-1-80199-789-8

2 4 6 8 10 9 7 5 3 1

Text design by Lauren Debono-Elliot

Printed and bound in Great Britain by Clays Ltd, Elcograf S.p.A.

To find out more about our authors and books visit
www.bloomsbury.com and sign up for our newsletters

For product safety related questions contact
*productsafety@bloomsbury.com*

# Contents

Welcome ..................................................... 9

Backstage ................................................. 10
Leap Year ................................................. 12
Bird .......................................................... 14
Poetic Licence ........................................... 16
Ponky Woem .............................................. 18
Saturday Morning ..................................... 20
At Home ................................................... 22
Take Care ................................................. 24
Somnolent Solomon Simon ....................... 26
Play Date .................................................. 27
My Dog ..................................................... 28
Aeroplane Impression ............................... 30
Butterfly Necklace .................................... 32
The Kiss .................................................... 34
A Promise ................................................. 36
My Pet Lemon ........................................... 38
Dad's Brags .............................................. 39
A Chef's Request ...................................... 40
Spicy Mind ................................................ 41
Knot What I Expected .............................. 42
As Scared As Me ...................................... 44
You Can't Take Away My Love ................. 46

| | |
|---|---|
| Kindergarten | 48 |
| Waiting for Lunch | 49 |
| Teachers Are Human Too | 50 |
| The Caretaker | 52 |
| Odd Job Man | 53 |
| Playgrounds in the Rain | 54 |
| If | 56 |
| Going Viral | 58 |
| Uncle Ian's Car | 59 |
| Racin' Rover | 60 |
| Catting Around | 62 |
| The Pets of Ukraine | 64 |
| Victoria Park | 66 |
| I Cannot Write a Poem | 68 |
| Gaps | 69 |
| Performance Art | 70 |
| Get Oeuvre It | 71 |
| I Can't Read Because | 72 |
| Making a Name For Myself | 73 |
| The Basher | 74 |
| Ouch! | 75 |
| Variety | 76 |
| Fly on the Wall | 77 |
| Fear of Flying | 78 |
| Walking | 80 |
| All You Can Eat | 82 |

| | |
|---|---|
| Got the Hump | 84 |
| Noah's ASK | 86 |
| Indoor Cat | 88 |
| Rubbish Poem | 90 |
| Going Wild | 92 |
| Counting on Me | 94 |
| It Was Like That When I Got There | 95 |
| Catching the Flakes | 96 |
| Towers | 98 |
| Ten Reasons Why I Shouldn't Go to Bed | 100 |
| Space Shorts | 102 |
| The Farthest Star | 104 |
| Defying the Odds | 106 |
| And So I Write | 108 |
| | |
| Acknowledgements | 111 |

## Welcome

Perhaps you are not feeling very awesome right now. That's OK. No one feels awesome all the time. In fact, lots of the time I don't feel awesome at all. Just like everyone, I sometimes feel anxious, upset, afraid. When I feel like this, one of the things I like to do is to write funny poems. I have included some of these poems in this book.

When I write, it helps me to feel a bit more awesome. Another thing that helps me when I'm feeling down is reading – funny stuff, yes, but also stuff that makes me think and reflect. I have included some of those types of poems in this book too.

When you read this book, I hope it helps calm the storm in your mind. It might make you laugh, it might make you think (or even cry), but my hope is that you come away feeling a bit better than you did before. The world can be a tricky place, but I think words, and poetry, can help us all feel just a little bit...awesome.

## Backstage

I'm waiting in the dressing room.
It is a most distressing room.
I listen to the chatter
and the creaking of the door.

My heart is pounding loudly now.
Although I'm standing proudly now,
my hands are getting clammy
and we're on at half past four.

The costumes hang on railings
as I contemplate my failings;
have I memorised my lines
or will the doubt be on display?

My talent will be plain to see!
The people will believe in me!
I tell myself I'm awesome
while my nerves begin to fray.

But when the lights grow dimmer
I can sense my spirit shimmer
as the sunshine in my mind
and in my body blazes through.

The curtains slowly come apart.
The spectacle's about to start.
Yes, this is where I'm meant to be –
it's what I'm born to do!

## Leap Year

**LEAP** at the thought
of a walk through the trees
**LEAP** at the swish
of a billowing breeze

**LEAP** at the prospect
of riding your bike
**LEAP** at the leeway
to leap as you like

**LEAP** at the sound
of the telly on loud
**LEAP** as you daydream
and stare at a cloud

**LEAP** over hedges,
through meadows and parks
**LEAP** at the notion
of leapingsome larks

**LEAP** at the sight
of your mates as they play
**LEAP** at the gift
of a whole extra day!

## Bird

A poem is like a bird.
Words poke their way
through the shell of your brain,
tentatively touching the page

with their baby beaks.
You build a nest for them,
feed them worms
so their bones grow strong.

Nursing them diligently,
you protect them from harm.
For a time you mustn't let
anyone approach,

lest their feathers snap
like twigs or their wings
wither and wilt away.
Night, however, turns to day

and with a guarded sigh
you watch your fledgling fly.

## Poetic Licence

I got me a Poetic Licence
and I ain't afraid to use it.

My Poetic Licence means I can
use words like 'ain't',
and no one can stop me.

My Poetic Licence means I don't
even have to use a full stop
at the end of this sentence
if I don't wanna

(I'm also allowed to use
words like 'wanna'.)

When I flash my Poetic Licence
they let me into buildings labelled
'Authenticity', 'Emotion'
and 'Artistry.

Other buildings won't let me in
unless I give up my Poetic Licence –
those places are named
things like 'Exams', 'Elitism'
and 'Conformity',

but I got me a Poetic Licence
and I ain't gonna hand it in
to no one.

See, my poetic Licence lets me
say things like this
at the end of a poem:

**SAUSAGES!**

Yeah I got me a Poetic Licence, dude,
and I ain't afraid to use it...

## Ponky Woem

I'm just a ponky woem
in a bonky little wook.
I know you sink it's thilly
but just lome and have a cook.

My bords are rather wackwards
and my stread is not on haight.
Yes mome sight steem me dupid
but en thothers gray I'm seat.

Ly mexicon jis umbled.
Ly metters are askew.
I know you wink I'm theird
but I'm gather rripping too.

I save to hay crim azy
and against all tommon caste.
I'm just a ponky woem
and sy mense bas heen pismlaced.

# Saturday Morning

I'll hop in a rocket
then shoot to the moon;
I'll set off for Saturn,
arriving by noon;
I'll put on my helmet
and count down from ten –
the places I'll go
when I pick up a pen.

I'll saunter through streets
in Victorian times,
cavorting with crooks
and committing some crimes;
I'll linger with thieves
as they lurk in their den –
the stuff that I'll see
when I pick up a pen.

I'll roam with the Romans,
geek out with the Greeks;
I'll train with some troopers,
discern their techniques,
then battle my demons
again and again –
the things that I'll do
when I pick up a pen.

I'll conjure a saviour,
loving and warm,
to help me escape
from my family storm;
I'll try to come home
but I cannot say when –
I'm simply too busy
alone with my pen.

## At Home

We sit in the stands
with our steaming cups of hot chocolate.
I ask if he thinks we'll win.
He says that we definitely won't.

I drink it all in –
the little men in the distance,
running up and down on the greenest grass I've ever seen;
the voice booming over the loudspeakers;
the scent of pie and beer.

He reaches into his pocket
and hands me a toffee,
the kind I'm not allowed at home.
'Don't tell your mum', he says.

We lose.

And there it is – my first ever football match.
A bitter winter's evening;
a two-nil defeat
and Grandpa's hand, so warm in mine
as we walk across the windswept park.

## Take Care

Take care of the flowers.
Although you can't see their colours right now,
they'll be waiting for you
when you return.

And mend the roof.
Right now you're drenched
from lashings of rain,
but the time will soon come

when you finally step
into the warmth.
A shelter will be waiting for you,
and the beautiful colours outside.

Take care now, even though
it all feels empty, hopeless.
Good things await you,
and you will see that life is good.

## Somnolent Solomon Simon

I'm Somnolent Solomon Simon.
I loiter and linger and laze.
I stretch and I sprawl
doing nothing at all,
lackadaisically wasting my days.

My body's beset by inertia.
My soul's soporifically still.
In vigour I'm lacking,
but slothfully slacking
I guess you could say is my skill.

Yes I'm perfectly, pleasantly passive.
I'm partial to taking my time.
As I drift in my dreams
I'm so sleepy it seems
that I shan't even finish this rh

## Play Date

He hogs all my toys
and he rushes around.
He stamps with his feet
and he spits on the ground.

He's scatty and tatty
and slathered with snot.
He says he's the boss
though I tell him he's not.

We sit in the sandpit:
I'm covered in sand.
He snatches the ice cream
straight out of my hand.

He jumps off the sofa
and teases the cat.
He bites and he burps
and behaves like a brat.

I've never met someone
with manners as poor –
I don't think I'll play
with my dad anymore.

## My Dog

My dog is very valiant,
adventurous and brave.
He's climbed the highest mountain
and explored the darkest cave.
His appetite for escapades
is difficult to sate.
The lure of deadly enterprises
simply won't abate.

My dog has battled dragons
and defeated evil beasts.
He's turned the toughest creatures
into rich and tasty feasts.
The streets are always empty
when he's out and on the prowl.
He'll make you wet your underpants
with nothing but a growl.

My dog is temerarious
and brilliantly bold.
The level of his courage
is amazing to behold.
He's mighty and he's muscular
but here's the caveat:
there's just one thing that frightens him
and that thing is

my cat.

## Aeroplane Impression

I hate it when Dad
does his aeroplane impression.

I'll be sitting there, feeling grumpy
about school or an argument with friends,

and Dad starts doing this flappy thing
with his lips - brbrbrbrbrbrbrbrbrrbrbr -

I try to ignore him, but the noise
keeps going -
brbrbrbrbrbrbrbrbrrbrbrbrbrbrbrbrbrbrbrrbrbr -

I tell him to stop, but the sound
gets even louder -
BRBRBBBBRBBRBRBRBRBRBRRRBBR! -

and it keeps on going -
BRBRBBBBRBBRBRBRBRBRBRRRBBR!!! -
and he starts running around the living room,

his lips buzzing like a crazy propeller,
his arms outstretched like stupid wings,

and maybe, just maybe, I'll begin to laugh.
Or at least smile. And then, if I'm feeling up to it,

if the mood somehow takes me,
if I can bear to leave my troubles behind,

I'll clamber aboard Dad's back.
He'll hold me in place with those big safe hands

and maybe, just maybe,
we both might fly.

## Butterfly Necklace

She said the necklace came
from her own mother, who got it
from someone else before the war.

She hid it safely in her pocket
when they had to get away.
Through the long nights and endless days,

through all those different countries,
she kept the butterfly necklace close.
The necklace was made

of gold, with red and blue wings,
and she said she wore it so that
I'd remember something of her

when she'd gone. And when she flew
off, like a butterfly through the summer
sun, that necklace was what

was left; the butterfly necklace –
red, blue and gold – that sits soft
and heavy on my chest.

## The Kiss

When my grandma gave me a kiss
she always used to say
that I wasn't allowed to rub it off.

She'd peck me on the cheek,
or the forehead, and my hand
would rise instinctively

to wipe away the wet.
"Hey!" she'd say.
"Don't wipe my kiss away!"

And so I'd go around all day
trying not to touch my face,
leaving the kiss where it was

until eventually it would seep into
my skin, becoming one with my body.
I'd carry the kiss wherever I went.

Now I've nothing left to lug but my tears.
I catch my hand rising once again
to dab away the damp

and I stop myself. I leave it be –
like the kisses, the tears
are all a part of me.

# A Promise

When the corners of your life jab into your chest
When you're drowning in all your options
When a thought takes on the weight of a mountain
and a mountain is invisible through the thicket of your thoughts
When a washing machine churns in your stomach
When your ribs are made of matchsticks
When the soundtrack of your mornings
is an out of tune guitar
When your food tastes of the tissues

that have melted in your tears
When your years condense to minutes
and a minute lasts for years
When all your clothes are loose and creased
and you wear your bones like armour
When the voices in your head heckle you
When your breath is smoke
When they laugh at your beliefs
and they frown at your joke
When the sandwiches in your picnic are filled with hair
I'll be there. I'll listen. I'll care.

## My Pet Lemon

I took a lemon home today
to keep me company –
an idiosyncratic pet,
I'm sure you will agree.

It has a waxy yellow coat.
It's got a leafy stem on.
It doesn't really do a lot –
just sits there like a lemon.

## Dad's Brags

My darling is a genius.
She taught herself to read.
She also plays the violin
and swims at super speed.

She's quite the whizz at ballet
and she's excellent at chess.
When asked about her aptitude
one has to acquiesce.

She knows her Dickens off by heart.
She cooks delicious food.
With high degrees of giftedness
my girl has been imbued.

She's got the knack for algebra
though she is only three.
My darling is a genius.
She sure takes after me.

# A Chef's Request

I can't stand jalapeños.
Please keep them out my pot.
They're jarrowingly jorrible
and jideously jot!

# Spicy Mind

I have a spicy mind. It doesn't
do what people tell it to.
It's often very friendly but then
sometimes it'll yell at you.
It's like a pair of horses pulling
each their separate way at once,
or else a jumping jester with
a chestful of annoying stunts.

I have a spicy mind. It often
makes me want to scream and shout.
It's like a tiger, locked up in
a cage, that simply can't get out.
It throws me lots of curveballs
and it's riddled with anxiety.
It conjures ways to trick me
with its impish impropriety.

I have a spicy mind. I guess
it's tiring, but I've grown to learn
that often it's delectable
despite the way my brain can burn.
My mind belongs to me, you see
I think I might be stuck with it,
so stick it in your recipe
and come and try your luck with it!

## Knot What I Expected

Sometimes I sit
and I think that my mind
is a bit like a pretzel –

positive thoughts twisting
and turning to become negative
ones; each thought doubting

itself and all the others;
no ending or resolution, just round
and round in doughy loops...

At times like these,
the best thing to do?
Why not have a biscuit instead.

## As Scared As Me

Somewhere,
perhaps in a bedroom across the world,
sits a boy as scared as me.

He doesn't know me
and I don't know him,
but I'm sure he's there.

His brow is sweaty just like mine,
and as with me, tears prick at his eyes.
I can't tell my parents

and he can't tell his.
We are each alone,
yet connected in our fear.

I stretch out my arm
around this planet we call home,
and I hold the boy's hand.

I feel its warmth, its grip.
I feel his blood pumping.
He doesn't know me

and I don't know him,
yet here we are,
holding each other's loneliness.

## You Can't Take Away My Love

You can take away the hairs
From the top of my head
You can take away my butter
Along with my bread
You can make me sleep
On a prison bed
But you can't take away my love

You can fill my brain
With a tangle of doubt
You can toy with my mind
Til I want to shout
But I'll tell you what it is
That I'm all about –
You can't take away my love

You can take the shirt
Right off my back
You can put my belongings
In your sack
Record all my failings
In an almanac
But you can't take away my love

You can give me a zero
On your swanky test
You can bang a hammer
Inside my chest
But it doesn't matter
See, I've been blessed
Cos you can't take away my love
No you can't take away my love

# Kindergarten

I'm a stegosaurus, I told her.
She replied that a real stegosaurus
wouldn't know it was a stegosaurus,
still less would it be able
to articulate the fact.

We weren't friends after that.

# Waiting for Lunch

My stomach is empty.
I'm waiting for lunch –
a sandwich, some crisps
and an apple to crunch.

I've opened my book
but my brain's feeling dense;
the words and the numbers
are not making sense.

The clock isn't moving.
My tummy is growling.
The lesson is boring.
My insides are howling.

I wish I could eat
and then play on the grass!
I guess I'll just have to
keep teaching my class.

## Teachers Are Human Too

They cook, they clean
They read, they dream
They eat ice cream
Teachers are human too

They sing and clap
They jog, they nap
(With dog on lap)
Teachers are human too

They laze about
They preen, they pout
They're full of doubt
Teachers are human too

They make a brew
They're just like you
They sometimes even
Use the loo

(It's true!)

Because teachers
Are human too.

## The Caretaker

takes care of the windows
and care of the floors
care of the car park
and care of the doors

care of the dustbins
and care of the walls
care of the playground
and care of the halls

care of the fixtures
and fittings and locks
care of the toilets
and care of the clocks

care of the building
with never a fuss
and care of the school
that takes care of us.

# Odd Job Man

I get my wage
in different ways –
I juggle fish
for days and days;
I ride on bears;
mend roofs with eggs;
I paint on wasps
and swallow pegs.

I earn my keep
by knitting bricks;
I make alarm clocks
with some sticks;
I cuddle snakes
and dance with spoons;
I comfort elves
and fight balloons.

For cash in hand
I'll tickle mice
and cook a car
with lots of spice.
I'm an Odd Job Man –
it's strange but true.
Odd jobs are what
I'm paid to do.

## Playgrounds in the Rain

I like playgrounds in the rain –
everyone indoors, at home or work
or school. Just me and Dad,

him in his yellow raincoat
and me in my big green wellies.
No queues to use the swings

or slide – I have the whole thing
to myself. Dad sits with his coffee
and his hood up as I play.

I like the quiet. I like the way
each raindrop sanctifies this place.
Dad smiles beneath his yellow hood;

although the sky is gristle grey
it wraps me in its arms somehow.
I sit on the see-saw; no one but me –

I wallow in my gravity,
and as the clouds converge above
I take a breath

and know I'm free.

## If

If you were a radio
I'd listen to you all day.

If you were a pair of shoes
I'd walk with you everywhere.

If you were a chocolate bar
I'd savour your flavour forever.

If you were a pillow
I'd bury my face in your softness.

If you were a tree
I'd get to know the wisdom of your years.

If you were a bird
I'd build my nest with you.

If you were a road
I'd find out where you lead.

If you were the stars
I'd capture the whole night sky.

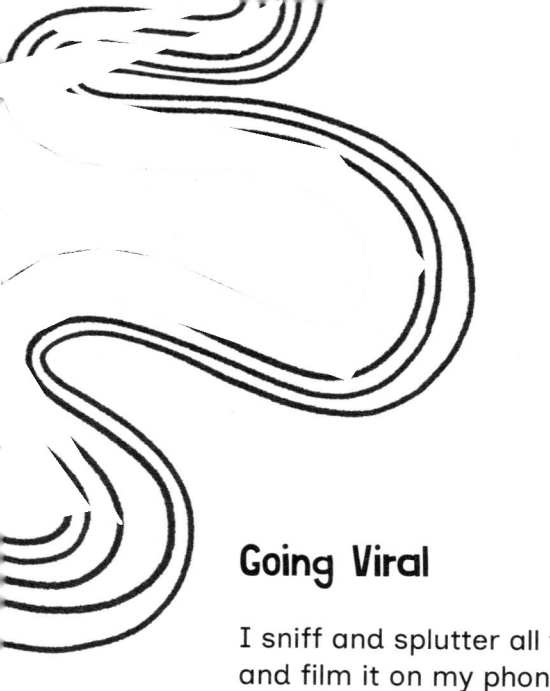

## Going Viral

I sniff and splutter all the time
and film it on my phone.
The people flock to see me cough
and watch me writhe and moan.

My arms and legs get achey
while I put it all online.
My following keeps growing
as I shiver, shake and whine.

My temperature's as high
as all my likes on Instagram.
An influenza influencer –
that is what I am.

# Uncle Ian's Car

Dad wakes me up in the middle of the night.
He hoists me out of bed. We go outside.
Uncle Ian has a new car.

He sits me in the driver's seat.
That's the gear stick. There's the clutch.
He isn't sure what this button does.

Later that night, I lie in bed.
Ian and Dad, they're talking downstairs.
Slowly, softly, sleep takes over –

I'm driving on rainbows,
the clouds in my hair.

## Racin' Rover

My dog is a lethargic beast.
His need for speed is slight,
until he sees a squirrel, then

hedashesoutofsight.

He shuffles slowly up the path.
His lassitude is stark,
until he sees a squirrel, then

hehurtlesroundthepark.

When up against his indolence
few others can compete,
until he sees a squirrel, then

hezoomsacrossthestreet.

My dog is chilled, my dog is calm,
his coolness can't be faulted,
until he sees a squirrel, then

hesimplycan'tbehaltedddddddd!!

# Catting Around

I'm catting around
Just catting around

Might sleep through day
On a soft settee
Have a stretch, have a yawn
Lick my bum, scratch a flea
Might stare at a bird
Might lunge at a mouse
Might drink from the sink
As I slink round the house

Cos I'm catting around
Yeah catting around

I'll climb on your face
When you're trying to sleep
I'll lounge on your bed
In a soft, furry heap
Might sit on your book
Get hair on the couch
Might act like a clown
Might sulk like a grouch

Cos I'm catting around
Just catting around

See I'm a good little kitty
When I wanna be nice
But I have a few words
So I'll keep it precise:
Might bat your head
Might sit on your chest –
It's *my* place now
So be a good guest

While I'm catting around
Yeah while I'm catting around.

## The Pets of Ukraine

Through bombed out streets,
across rickety bridges,
we carry our cats and dogs

like crosses, some held aloft
in cardboard boxes, others
wrapped in scarves and coats.

And as we pick out our way
through the debris and smoke
we cling on to them

and clasp them close,
knowing we'd no more
leave them behind than

our own children.
Their breath, their hearts –
they're part of us, for as long

as there are cats and dogs
there's still much more
that's right than wrong.

## Victoria Park

A little girl
asks another little girl
how old she is.

A Siberian Husky
watches two burly men
feed nuts to a squirrel.

Boys play basketball
as mums converse
in foreign tongues.

Sometimes, you know,
things aren't quite
so bad.

# I Cannot Write a Poem

I cannot write a poem.
It's something I can't do.
To say I am incapable
is definitely true.

I do not have proficiency.
I lack the brains and skill.
Whenever I sit down to type
it always goes downhill.

Yes, poetry's beyond me.
Ineptitude's my curse.
I can't create a simple rhyme
or write a single verse.

I frankly cannot do it,
however hard I try.
I didn't write this poem –
it was written by AI.

# Gaps

Love lives in the gaps.
In the spaces between hatred and envy,
between jealousy and disgust,
between bitterness and rage –
is that a tender green shoot?

In the gaps between machines,
in the dank corners of the warehouse
packed to its roof with automata –
does something softly smile?

Love lives where computers aren't.
It thrives on no file,
can be held by no phone,

and the greyer the world gets,
the more precious the gemstones.

## Performance Art

Well it's not in a gallery
and it's not a painting.

You've sold no tickets
and no one knows it's happening.

It's simply the case
that you're sat here

breathing,

creating something beautiful.

## Get Oeuvre It

My navel comprises a novel.
A haiku's on top of my head.
My fibula fizzles with fiction.
My feet trail facts where I tread.

A sonnet is sat on my shoulder.
My nose is composed of some odes.
There's an atlas attached to my anke.
A symphony lives in my nodes.

My limbs, they consist of a limerick.
I guess you could call it a quirk.
My liver is literally literature –
I've got quite a body of work.

## I Can't Read Because...

I'm seriously sick,
unusually unwell,

powerfully poorly,
awfully afflicted,

grimly grotty,
really rather ropey;

I've a dastardly debilitation –
a bad case of alliteration.

## Making a Name for Myself

My moniker is Monica.
From Monaco I came.
I'm good on the harmonica;
Veronica's the same.

They ask about my moniker.
"It's Monica", I claim,
"and me and my Veronica,
we came in search of fame."

My moniker is Monica.
Simplicity's my aim:
see, Monica's my moniker –
my name's the name for 'name'.

## The Basher

They call me The Basher.
They shudder with fright.
Just mention my moniker:
flocks will take flight.

My epithet's famous
to all in the town.
Refer to 'The Basher'
and pants will turn brown.

When told I'm approaching
they tremble with fear;
they burble and babble
"The Basher is here."

My name is so dreaded
it's hard to believe.
They call me The Basher...
But Mum calls me 'Steve'.

## Ouch!

Monty McGonagall's
comical monocle
sat on his face
when he started to cry,

for Monty McGonagall's
monocle's conical,
liable therefore
to jab in his eye.

(And that is the end of
this monocle chronicle,
therefore I bid you
a pointed goodbye.)

# Variety

is the spice of life, they say.
Well I don't really like spicy things.
When I come home to the same warm
bed every night –
that's the stuff I like.
The same table, chairs and cutlery
waiting for me at breakfast –
I like that.
A different set of shoes in the hallway;
some other car in the driveaway;
a new school every few years –
that's the stuff that burns
in the back of my throat.
Variety might be the chilli flakes,
but I want the solid stuff, the nourishment.
I need the potatoes, the chicken, the rice –
the things that fill up a life.

# Fly on the Wall

People sometimes wish
to be a fly upon the wall.

They think that this would help
to grow their knowledge overall.

I do not think, however,
it would be much use at all –

the thing about a fly is that
its brain is rather small.

# Fear of Flying

I've got a fear of flying.
It causes me to fret.
To see the ground beneath me
makes me break out in a sweat.

It leaves me feeling giddy.
My stomach starts to heave.
The scope of my revulsion
isn't easy to conceive.

I've sought help from a therapist.
It didn't do the trick.
Whenever I am airborne
I get bilious and sick.

You may contend it's normal
but this crisis is absurd –
the thing is, my aversion
isn't great when you're a bird.

## Walking

Go for a walk, they say.
Keep moving. Keep active.

The problem is

my mind is always moving;
my brain is always active.

I'm always walking inside my own head.

Step after
      step after
           step after
                  step.

See,

maybe I need to slow down.
Maybe we need to stop walking.

# All You Can Eat

I gobbled a pizza
and beans from a tin.
I slurped a rice pudding
and savoured the skin.

I snaffled a sausage
with bacon and eggs.
I wolfed down a schnitzel
and ten chicken legs.

The size of the portions
adorning my plate
might cause you to wonder
if things will abate.

I feasted on pasta,
potatoes and peas.
I chomped on chorizo
and churros and cheese.

I then had some biscuits
and tea from a cup,
but I think it's enough now –
I'm feeling fed up.

# Got the Hump

If you're feeding
a camel
then ham'll
be edgy,

and lamb'll
be dodgy
and clam'll
be wrong;

a yam'll
be better
since camels
are veggie,

but mammals
get podgy
if fed
for too long.

## Noah's ASK

I've got a bunch of questions.
There's a lot I'd like to know,
like can you make a mala**MUTE**
and where does flamin**GO**?
What made the cormo**RANT**,
I ask, and is the marmo**SET**?
Why is the casso**WARY**?
Does it need to see a vet?

There is some information
that I really wish were mine,
like could a labra**DOODLE**
and why does a porcu**PINE**?
Where did the ant**ELOPE**
and do you think the peli**CAN**?
When the weather's very sunny
will it make orangu**TAN**?

Of all the learning in the world
there's loads I really need,
like does a cocka**POO**
and where on earth has centi**PEDE**?
Who turned the baboo**ON**?
Oh yes, and can the butter**FLY**?
Such queries make me peckish
so I'll munch on a mag**PIE**.

## Indoor Cat

She's an indoor cat.
Her world lies within the walls
of our first floor flat.
She sits at the window
eyeing the birds outside,
creatures she will never catch.
Her exercise routine is walking
from the kitchen to the bedroom and back.
She's an indoor cat.
The rug is her Serengeti,
the couch her habitat.
Excitement, for her, is a post to scratch.

She's never brought home a frog or a rat.
And is she happy?
Well it's all she's ever known.
Her whole universe
is circumscribed by our home.
Her eyes are keen.
Her claws are sharp
but she knows no combat.
Just look at her there –

She's an indoor cat.

## Rubbish Poem

I picked up a puppy.
My tenth of the day.
It's tiny and newborn
and fluffy and grey.

The reason I'm holding
this lovable critter –
my mum and dad told me
to pick up the litter.

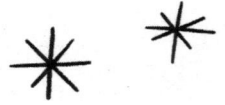

## Going Wild

There's a lemur on my lunchbox,
a bonobo on my book,
and a snake inside my pencil case –
just come and have a look!

There's a rhino on my rucksack
while a chimp sits in my chair.
There's a panther with my paper
prowling proudly to its lair.

A chinchilla nabbed my dinner,
an alpaca my protractor;
a hyena, looking meaner,
got so close I nearly whacked her!

There's a tiger on my tabletop
(I promise you it's true)
and a cheetah ate my teacher
in our lesson at the zoo.

## Counting on Me

I counted a sequence
from **One** onto **Two**,
then **Three**, **Four** and **Five**
came up next in the queue.

**Six**, **Seven** and **Eight**
followed up on the list
then I hit upon **Nine**,
but the next one I missed.

The digits accrued
reached their limit somehow;
my tallying skills
are un**Ten**able now.

# It Was Like That When I Got There

*after Homer Simpson*

The telly's lying on its side
The shards of glass are hard to hide
The window's smashed, the hole is wide
But it was like that when I got there.

Tomato stains are on the rug
And sparks are flying from the plug
It wasn't me who chipped the mug –
It was like that when I got there.

The goldfish isn't in her bowl
The hamster's going for a stroll
My shoes have dog dirt on the sole
But it was like that when I got there.

The vase has fallen from the shelf
I know you left me by myself
But it must have been some sort of elf –
It was like that when I got there!

## Catching the Flakes

Today is a waterfall of sludge.
I'm at the river's edge
covered in mud,
a sieve in my hand.

I stand by the waterfall
trying to catch the flakes,
those tiny bits of gold that remind me
today hasn't been all grim.

See, I wrote part of a poem;
I walked the dog –
I catch these flakes in my sieve,
letting the rest of the day's muck

tumble on down to get washed
away by the river.
Tomorrow might be better,
I tell myself,

as I put the flakes in my bag,
dry myself off
and head softly, silently
into the night.

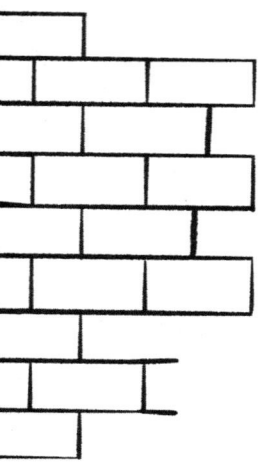

## Towers

My grandpa
used to build towers
in the living room.

Stacking the bricks
on top of each other,
I'd implore him
to make it go higher
and higher.

My brother said
he cheated,
because the tower
was on a table.

All that mattered to me
was that it touched
the ceiling.

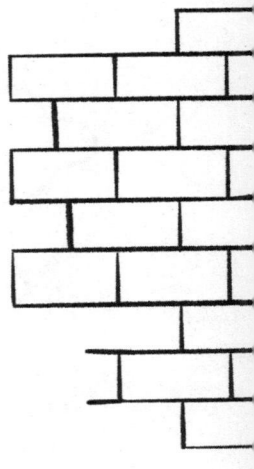

# Ten Reasons Why I Shouldn't Go to Bed

(1) There is some kind of yeti in my room. It's been threatening me.
(2) I've been studying philosophy, and I'm not even sure if my bed exists anyway.
(3) Sleep is for the weak, and I am strong, from which it follows that sleep is impossible. It's a simple matter of logic.
(4) James from school says you swallow spiders when you sleep. I don't want to swallow a spider.
(5) I found out that I have a deadly disease - beditis - which means that I am allergic to beds.

**(6)** I'm afraid that Joshua Seigal might slap me with a wet fish while I'm sleeping. Poets are weird like that.

**(7)** This television programme about donkeys is just sooooo interesting.

**(8)** Oh, I forgot to say, our topic for the whole this year is donkeys! I need to watch this programme!

**(9)** I need to stay up so I can write a letter explaining how much I love you. Did I ever tell you how much I love you?

**(10)**.......I'M NOT TIRED!!!!

## Space Shorts

I bought some new shorts
and I sped into space.
I shot past the planets
and relished the pace.

I dashed through the galaxy,
all round the stars.
My jet-powered shorts
drove me on via Mars.

I zipped and I zoomed
but I came to a halt.
I suddenly stopped
with a judder and jolt.

No words can express
the frustration I felt –
my shorts were held up
by an asteroid belt.

## The Farthest Star

Like the farthest star,
it was only once you'd gone
that I saw your light.

## Defying the Odds

They told her she couldn't.
She showed them a way.
They gave her directions.
She wandered astray.

They claimed that she mustn't.
She focused her gaze
and she carried on forward,
her pupils ablaze.

They opened the book
and they quoted statistics;
she conjured a set
of opposing logistics.

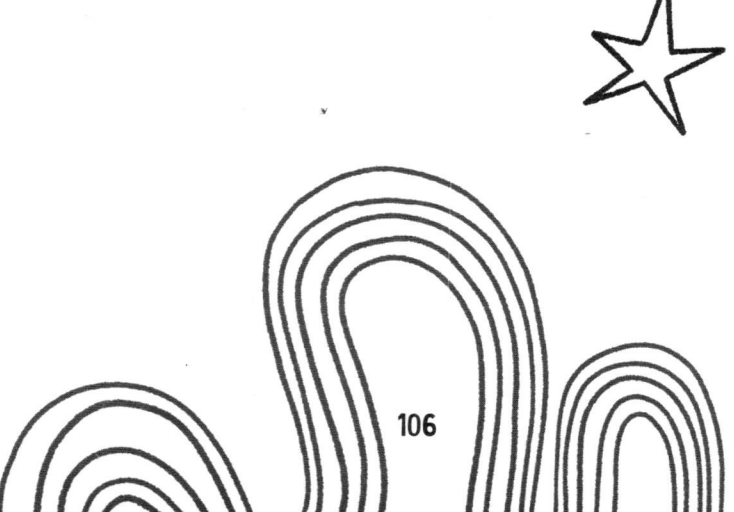

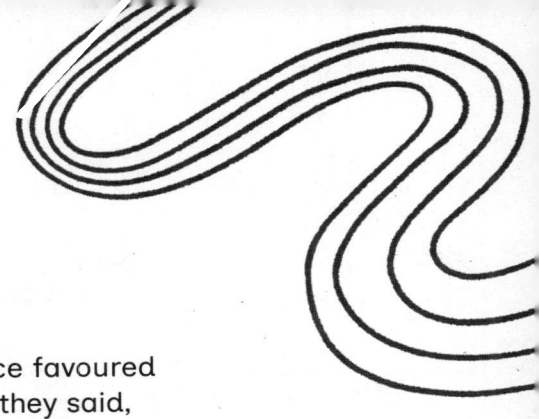

The evidence favoured
her failure, they said,
but she knew that the evidence
lay in her head.

The world turned against her.
She started to smile,
for idiosyncracy
suited her style.

She isn't a spirit,
nor one of the gods –
she's flesh and she's blood
and defying the odds.

## And So I Write

the word LOVE in my diary, to remind myself
of the underpinning of all the things I do.
I craft the letters with a ruler,

taking great pains to ensure that everything
is smooth, straight, in order. I decorate the word
with a border and I colour it all in, in a way

I haven't done since primary school.
I really want this word to stand out – LOVE.
The unassailable axiom; the uncaused cause;

that than which nothing greater can be conceived.
Until I realise that the letters aren't quite even.
Some of the lines are thicker than others

and if you squint a bit you can see
a slight smudge on the page. The letter O
seems sort of squished, and although the word

is still, recognisably, LOVE, it looks somewhat
misformed, somehow. And so I carry now
this buckled LOVE everywhere I go –

in my diary, tucked tight in my rucksack –
and this imperfection is part of everything I do,
a bold, flawed LOVE on the pages of my days.

## Check out Joshua Seigal's other poetry collections for more awesome mood boosts!

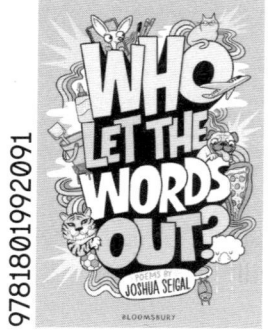

9781801992091

9781472972743

9781472972729

9781472955487

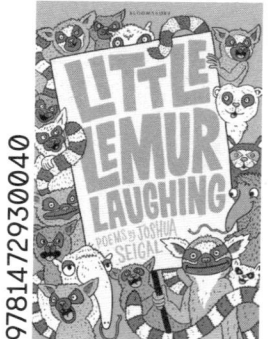

9781472930040

9781472930033

# Acknowledgements

'Butterfly Necklace' won Second Place in the 2023 Caterpillar Poetry Prize, judged by Michael Rosen.

'Defying the Odds' first published on Forward Arts Foundation website.

'And So I Write' first published in Cosy Poems (ed. Gaby Morgan), Macmillan 2024.